curvy girl for the best friend

emma bray

one

. . .

Jake

THE SUN BEATS down on the playground as I race Lily to the jungle gym. Her long blonde hair whips behind her as she sprints ahead, laughing. At eight years old, she's already faster than me.

"Eat my dust, Jakey!" She sticks out her tongue and scrambles up the metal bars.

"No fair, you got a head start!" I protest, chasing after her.

We spend the afternoon playing make-believe—explorers discovering new lands, pirates hunting for treasure. With Lily, anything seems possible. She has the boldest imagination of anyone I know.

As the light fades, we collapse in the grass, out of breath but grinning.

"We'll be best friends forever, right Jake?" Lily turns her sky-blue eyes to mine.

"Forever and ever," I nod solemnly. "I pinky promise."

Our little fingers lock, sealing the vow. In this moment, I can't imagine ever being apart from her.

---

10 Years Later

Jake

"Oh my god, did you see Josh today? He looked sooo cute in that blue shirt..." Lily gushes to me as we walk home from school. With her long legs and cascade of golden hair, she's turned into the girl every guy wants. Every guy except the one she spends all her time with—her best friend. Me.

I nod along to her chatter, trying to ignore the clench in my chest. Lily's been my entire world for the past decade. But lately, my feelings have started to shift into decidedly un-friendly territory.

I catch myself staring at the swell of her breasts under her tank top, the tantalizing strip of skin when her shirt rides up. My mind wanders to forbidden fantasies.

Lily naked and writhing under me, panting my name...

"Jake? Hello?" She waves a hand in front of my face. "You still with me? I was just saying Josh smiled at me in Chem today. Do you think he might ask me to prom?"

"I don't know, Lil." I force lightness into my tone. "I guess we'll have to wait and see."

Later that night, I stroke my cock, images of Lily flickering behind my closed lids. Tears of shame prick my eyes as I muffle my groans into my pillow.

Why can't she look at me that way? I'm the one who's been here all along. I know her better than anyone.

But I can never tell her. I'd rather have Lily as a friend than risk losing her completely. Even if it means silently dying inside as I watch her fall for someone else.

———

Years pass, but my feelings for Lily only intensify. She remains as oblivious as ever, confiding in me about every crush and breakup. Each time her heart shatters, she ends up in my arms, sobbing onto my shoulder.

"I'll never understand men," she sobs. "Why do they always leave in the end?"

"It's not you, Lily," I assure her, biting back the bitter truth. "You just haven't found the right one yet."

I offer her a tissue, a muscle twitching in my jaw. I know I'm lying to her face—the right one's been right in front of her this entire time. And it kills me to know she'll never see me that way.

Lily dries her eyes and gives me a hug. "Thanks, Jake. I don't know what I'd do without you."

Neither do I, I think grimly, as I hug her back, inhaling her sweet vanilla scent. Because without Lily, I'd be nothing. But I swallow my feelings down, burying them deep inside, where they can't hurt anyone—especially not her.

As time goes on, Lily's relationships become a blur. One arrogant jerk after another, each one breaking her heart in a slightly different way. Guys who don't deserve someone as perfect as my Lily.

Thank fuck she's still a virgin. I'm her best friend, so she tells me everything, and she has yet to let any of the losers she dates pop her perfect little cherry.

It's a good thing too because I don't know what I'd do if someone did. Probably go to jail for homicide.

I'm not even sure when my protectiveness turns to something darker, more possessive. All I know is that when I see another guy touching her, my fists clench involuntarily, and I have to watch my words lest I scare her away.

But I can't help it. Lily's *mine*—even if she doesn't know it yet.

One day, I'm going to reach my breaking point. I've had enough of watching her date loser after loser, each one treating her like a trophy rather than the precious gift she is.

Lily's crying again, and I can't take it anymore. I pull her close, wrapping her in a hug, my body aching for hers.

If only I could tell her how I really feel…

two

. . .

Jake

I WATCH as Lily laughs with her date across the bar, his hand resting casually on her thigh. The sight makes my blood boil. I clutch my beer bottle so hard my knuckles turn white.

My heart clenches painfully in my chest, suffocating me from the inside out. I love her so damn much. Have since we were just kids playing in her backyard. But I'm a coward—too afraid to tell her how I really feel. To risk losing even the simple pleasure of her friendship if she rejects me.

Lily throws her head back, blonde curls cascading down her back as she laughs at something he said. Her blue eyes sparkle with joy. God, she's so beautiful it hurts to look at her sometimes. I want to pull her into my arms and never let go. To finally confess the depths of my feelings, consequences be damned.

But I remain frozen in place, the words lodged in my throat. Some man I am, too chickenshit to tell the woman I love how I feel.

Her date's hand slides higher up her thigh and something in me snaps. White hot jealousy rips through me like a bullet. I can't do this anymore. Can't sit back and watch her fall for someone else over and over while I pine away in the shadows like a lovesick fool.

I abruptly get up from my stool, legs unsteady. I have to get out of here before I do something stupid like punch that douchebag in the face. Or finally blurt out my feelings to Lily in a jealous, drunken confession.

No, what I need is a real escape. A fresh start, far away from here.

Far away from *her*. Just the thought makes my heart ache, but I know what I have to do.

With grim determination, I walk out of the bar and don't look back.

Tomorrow, I'm going to the recruitment office and signing up for the marines. I can't stay in this town a minute longer watching the woman I love move on without me. It's time I move on too.

———

The sun beats down on my neck as I make my way up Lily's driveway, each step heavier than the last. My duffel bag feels like it weighs a ton, but it's nothing compared to the weight in my chest.

I raise my hand to knock, but the door swings open before I can.

And there she is. Lily. My best friend. The love of my life. The one I'm leaving behind.

"Jake..." She breathes my name, blue eyes already shimmering with unshed tears. "I can't believe you're really leaving."

I swallow hard, fighting to keep my own emotions in check. "Gotta do what I gotta do, Lil."

She nods, worrying her bottom lip between her teeth. A habit she's always had when she's upset or anxious. I want so badly to reach out and smooth away the furrow between her brows. To pull her into my arms and never let go.

But I don't. I *can't*. Not if I want to keep my resolve and walk away.

"I'm proud of you, you know," she says softly, reaching out to straighten the collar of my uniform.

Her fingers linger and my breath hitches. "You're so brave, Jake. You're going to make an amazing Marine."

I'm not brave, I want to tell her. *I'm a coward. I'm running away from my feelings for you. From the possibility of you rejecting me and losing you forever.*

"Thanks, Lil," I manage to choke out instead. "That means a lot."

She bites her lip again, harder this time. "Promise me you'll be careful over there? That you'll come back home to me?"

To me. The words slam into my chest like a freight train. If only she knew how much I wish I was coming home to her in the way I really want.

"I promise," I vow solemnly, even as my heart cracks a little further. I'll always come back to her, even if it's just as her friend. Having a piece of Lily is better than not having her at all.

Unable to resist any longer, I drop my bag and pull her into a tight hug. She melts against me instantly, arms winding around my neck as she buries her face in my shoulder. I breathe her in deep, memorizing the sweet scent of her shampoo and the warm press of her curves. Committing every detail to memory to take with me.

"I'm going to miss you so much," she whispers

brokenly against my neck, dampness seeping into my skin from her tears.

I squeeze my eyes shut against the hot sting of my own. "I'll miss you too, Lil. More than you know."

We cling to each other desperately, as if we could stop time and stay in this moment forever if we just hold on tight enough. My heart pounds against hers and I wonder if she can feel it. If she knows it only beats for her.

But all too soon, she's pulling back, swiping at her wet cheeks. I reluctantly let her go, even as every fiber of my being protests the loss of contact.

This is it. The moment I've been simultaneously dreading and anticipating. My chance to finally lay it all on the line. To tell her that I love her, that I've always loved her. That she's the reason I breathe, the reason my heart beats.

I open my mouth...and nothing comes out. I'm choked by fear, paralyzed by the possibility of losing her.

"Well, I guess this is goodbye for now," Lily says with a wobbly smile, unknowingly shattering the moment. "Promise you'll write to me?"

"I promise," I rasp, the unspoken words burning like acid in my throat.

She raises up on her toes and brushes a soft kiss

to my cheek. It sears into my skin like a brand. "Goodbye, Jake. Stay safe."

"Goodbye, Lily."

With monumental effort, I force myself to pick up my bag and walk away from the only home I've ever known. The only woman I'll ever love.

I don't let myself look back, blinking furiously against the hot tears blurring my vision. Each step away from her carves another piece out of my heart, but I keep going.

As I climb into my truck, I glance up at the charm hanging from my rearview mirror. A little silver lily flower. Lily gave it to me years ago. My flower. I reach up and touch it reverently, the metal warmed by the sun.

"I love you, Lily," I whisper to the empty cab, the words tearing out of me. "I'll always love you."

Then I put the truck in drive and force myself to leave her behind. But even as the distance grows between us, I know she'll never be far from my mind or my heart.

I'm hers, whether she knows it or not. And I always will be.

three

. . .

Four Years Later

Jake

THE RELENTLESS SUN beats down on my back as sweat trickles between my shoulder blades beneath heavy fatigues. Sand clings to my boots, gritty and invasive, as I march in line with my fellow marines across the sweltering desert training field. Each rhythmic step, each bead of sweat, each labored breath is meant to force her from my mind...

But Lily remains stubbornly lodged in my thoughts, as permanent and essential as the blood pumping through my veins.

"Keep up that pace, Corporal!" the drill sergeant barks. "Your mind better be one hundred percent in this moment!"

If he only knew that no amount of grueling physical training can seem to sweat Lily out of my system. Every night I collapse onto my cot, body aching and drained, but thoughts of her soft curves, silky hair, and gentle touch flood my mind and set my blood on fire all over again.

Sleep only comes in fitful bursts.

When mail call rings out, my pulse quickens. I spot her looping handwriting on an envelope, and my hands tremble slightly as I tear into it back in the privacy of my bunk.

Dear Jake, I miss you terribly. The clinic keeps me busy, but I often catch myself drifting off, imagining what you must be doing at that very moment...

Her innocent words, meant to comfort and connect platonically as my childhood best friend, instead stoke the flames of my forbidden desire. I picture Lily in her snug scrubs, golden hair tied back, tending to a puppy with such sweet nurturing—the way I desperately wish she would tend to me. I yearn to feel her pressed against me, soothing the raw ache of how much I need her.

...I'm always here if you need to talk. I know the separation from home must be so hard. You can tell me anything. I'll be counting the days until I see you again. Yours always, Lily.

The longing to confess the true depths of my feelings is a constant throb, but I swallow the words. I can't risk losing Lily's friendship, the one pure and good thing anchoring me. Even if I have to shut my eyes and picture her beneath me, writhing in pleasure, as I take my hard cock in hand night after night.

With a low groan, I carefully tuck away her letter to reread until the paper is soft and the creases worn. Each word is a reminder of what I'm fighting for—my sweet Lily waiting for me. And a reminder of the secret burning love that both sustains me and threatens to consume me whole.

And then I pull my aching cock from my pants. I close my eyes and picture Lily in my mind's eyes.

I grip my throbbing shaft tightly, imagining it's Lily's soft hand wrapped around me instead as I start pumping with desperate need. God, the thought of her touching me so intimately has me leaking and pulsing.

I picture her angelic face gazing up at me with those luminous blue eyes, pink lips parted in awe as she explores my rigid length curiously. "Like this, Jake?" she asks breathlessly, stroking me root to tip. I hiss through clenched teeth, fighting the urge to explode.

I grip the base of my cock, squeezing hard to stave off my impending orgasm. Even in my fantasies, I can barely handle the thought of Lily's touch without losing control.

I imagine pulling her into my lap, her plush ass nestled against my raging hard-on. "Can you feel what you do to me, baby?" I growl in her ear. "How fucking hard you make me?"

She gasps and wiggles, the friction deliciously maddening. I slide my hands up to cup her heavy tits, thumbing her nipples.

My rough hands knead Lily's soft breasts through the thin fabric of her shirt. Her responsive nipples strain against my palms as she arches into my touch with a breathy moan.

"Jake," she whimpers. "I've wanted you for so long..."

"Fuck, Lily," I groan, my hips rocking up to grind my aching cock against her ass. "You have no idea how many nights I've laid awake, so goddamn hard, thinking about this. Thinking about making you mine."

I rip open her shirt, sending buttons flying, desperate to feel her smooth bare skin. She gasps as I roll and pinch her rosy nipples between my fingers. My other hand snakes down to pop the button of her jeans and delve inside.

"Oh god," Lily cries out when my fingers find the wet heat of her pussy. She's absolutely soaked through her panties. I nudge the fabric aside and slide a finger through her slick folds, circling her swollen clit.

"Always so fucking wet and ready for me, aren't you baby?" I work a thick finger inside her tight channel as my thumb strums her clit. She clenches hard around me, hips bucking wildly.

"Yes, Jake! Don't stop!" Her head thrashes side to side, hair wild and cheeks flushed a deep pink as I finger fuck her hard and fast.

I can feel her start to flutter around my driving

fingers. "That's it, Lily. Come for me. Wanna feel this sweet little pussy coming all over my fingers."

"Jakeee!" she wails as the orgasm crashes through her. Her pussy clamps down, gushing hot juices over my hand as she convulses in my arms.

I groan, my cock kicking against my abs, so fucking close. With a few more rough pumps of my fist, I explode, thick ropes of cum painting my chest and stomach.

Panting, I collapse back onto the bed, the intense climax bittersweet. Because when I open my eyes, Lily is gone. Just a fantasy that simultaneously keeps me going and rips me apart with longing.

I clean myself up and try to slow my racing heart. Two more months. Two more months and I'll be back home, holding the only woman I've ever loved in my arms again. But will I ever have the courage to risk our friendship and show her the true force of my desire? To make her mine in every way?

It terrifies me more than any battlefield I've faced. But as I drift off to sleep, it's Lily's smiling face behind my closed eyelids, her name a prayer on my lips.

four

. . .

Lily

I'M NEARLY VIBRATING with excitement as I wait for Jake at the airport. My best friend is finally coming home where he belongs.

I honestly don't know how I got by without him hear for so many years. He's always been my right-hand man. My shoulder to cry on.

The only person I can really depend on.

I don't know what madness seized him and made him sign up for the Marines. Jake was never one who dreamed of serving in the military. In fact, he'd always talked about being a lawyer, so four years ago when he told me he was going into the military, he threw me for a loop.

I wanted to beg him to stay, but what could I do? Jake has always been a supportive friend to me, and it was only right that I be the same for him.

But I'd be totally lying if I said I didn't miss him like crazy.

But now he's coming back.

I'm standing on my tiptoes, trying to see over the crowd when I finally spot him.

He smiles and throws up his arm when he spots me.

I squeal with joy as I run into his arms.

His scent envelops me like a warm blanket as I step into his strong embrace, my heart racing. After all these years, he still feels like home.

"I've missed you so much," I whisper into his neck, squeezing him tighter. Breathing in his familiar musk awakens a flurry of cherished memories from our childhood together.

Jake's muscular arms wrap securely around my curvy frame. "I've missed you too, Lil. More than you know."

His deep, husky voice sends shivers down my spine. We pull back slightly, hands still grasping each other's arms, drinking in the sight of one another.

Jake looks older, more rugged and handsome, but his expressive green eyes still reflect the tenderhearted boy I grew up loving as my dearest friend.

My lips curve into a bright smile. "I can't believe you're finally back! There's so much to catch up on."

"We have all the time in the world now," he grins, shouldering his army duffle. "Let me look at you...You're as beautiful as ever."

Heat rises to my cheeks at the compliment. Jake takes my hand, electricity sparking at his touch as always, and we stroll out of the airport together. My best friend is home at last. The ache that took residence in my heart the day he left finally begins to heal. With Jake by my side again, I feel complete, safe and purely happy.

Jake hugs me close as we walk, his strong arm draped possessively around my shoulders. The heat of his body seeps through my thin t-shirt, igniting a flush across my skin.

My curves mold perfectly against the hard planes of his muscular frame. I can't help but melt into his protective embrace, savoring the feel of him. It's like coming home.

Jake's hand slides down to the small of my back, fingers splaying across my spine. "God, it feels good to hold you again, Lil. I didn't realize just how much I needed this...needed you."

"Well, just promise me you'll never go away again," I say petulantly over a sudden catch in my voice.

God, I've *missed* him.

————

Jake

Wrapping my arms around Lily's lush curves feels like heaven and hell combined. My cock instantly hardens, straining against my jeans as I breathe in her sweet, intoxicating scent.

Fuck, I *want* her. I've always wanted her.

Having her pressed up against me, all soft and warm, is testing every ounce of my self-control. It takes everything in me not to crush my mouth to hers, to claim her lips in a brutal kiss and show her exactly what she does to me.

But I can't. Lily still sees me as her childhood best friend. She has no idea about the filthy, depraved fantasies I've had about her gorgeous body. About burying my cock deep inside her tight, wet heat until she screams my name.

I need to do this right. Take it slow. Make her fall for me, so I can finally make her mine in every way. Because now that I'm back, there's no fucking way I'm letting Lily go. She's always been the only woman for me. I was just too much of a coward to tell her before I left.

But seeing her again, holding her, I know I can't risk losing her to someone else. I'd rather die than watch Lily end up with another man. No, she's *mine*. She always has been. She just doesn't know it yet.

I plaster on a friendly smile, even as my heart pounds wildly and my dick throbs with barely contained lust. "I'm not going anywhere, Lil. Wild horses couldn't drag me away from you again," I vow to her.

Not when I'm on a mission to win her heart and get her into my bed, where she belongs. Where I plan to keep her—naked, satisfied, and thoroughly claimed. I'll do whatever it takes to make Lily mine completely.

five

. . .

Jake

THE WARM GLOW of the kitchen light illuminates Lily's face as she stands at the counter, humming softly while chopping vegetables for dinner. I lean against the doorframe, my eyes tracing the gentle curves of her body, desire simmering beneath my skin. "Need any help?" I ask, my voice lower than I intend.

Lily glances up, her blue eyes widening slightly as they meet mine. "Sure, if you want to set the table, that would be great."

I nod, moving closer to grab the plates from the cupboard above her head. As I reach up, my chest brushes against her back, and I hear her breath catch. The urge to wrap my arms around her curvy waist nearly overwhelms me. Instead, I murmur, "Smells delicious," before stepping away, plates in hand.

Setting the table, I strategically place our seats closer together than usual. When Lily brings over the food, our fingers graze as she hands me a serving bowl. I hold her gaze a moment longer than necessary, trying to convey the depth of my feelings without words.

I don't know if Lily senses the shift in energy between us, but her cheeks flushing a delicate pink as she quickly turns back to the stove. Lily chatters about her day at the vet clinic, but I'm only half-listening, too distracted by the way her lips move and the tiny glimpses of cleavage visible above her low-cut top.

"So, how was your flight?" she asks as she plates up our food.

I clear my throat, trying to focus on the conversation and not the way her shirt stretches tightly across her breasts as she leans forward. "It was long. Bumpy. I couldn't stop thinking about getting back here the whole damn time," I say, my voice rough with barely restrained desire.

Lily's eyes flick up to meet mine and she pauses,

her hand frozen in midair. "Oh? That's...I'm glad you made it back safely." She swallows hard and I watch the delicate muscles of her throat move.

I want to press my lips there against her neck, tasting her soft skin as she gasps and tilts her head back. Instead, I take a sip of water, trying to cool the heat raging inside me.

"Thanks. It's good to be home," I say, my voice strained. "I missed...this. Us, hanging out." The unspoken "you" hangs heavy in the air between us.

"I missed you too, Jake," Lily beams at me before she places our plates on the table.

"Voila!" she announces. "Your first home-cooked meal since you've been back!"

I smile, my heart warming at her girlish enthusiasm. It's one of the many things I love about her. "Looks great, Lil."

Lily

As we sit down to eat, I can't help but notice how close Jake is sitting. His knee gently bumps mine under the table, sending a surprising tingle up my thigh. I glance at him, but he seems focused on his plate.

"This tastes amazing, Lil," he says after a few bites. "You've always been an incredible cook."

I feel a flush of pleasure at his compliment. "Thanks. It's nothing special, just something I threw together."

Jake sets down his fork, his green eyes intense as they meet mine. "Don't sell yourself short. You're special, Lily. Everything you do is extraordinary."

His words hang in the air between us, heavy with unspoken meaning. My heart beats faster, a confused mix of emotions swirling in my chest. This is Jake, my best friend, but something feels different now. The way he looks at me, the subtle shift in his tone...it's almost as if...

No. I shake my head slightly, pushing the thought away. He's just readjusting to being back home after so long away. I force a smile, trying to lighten the suddenly charged atmosphere. "Well, I learned from the best. Remember all those cooking lessons your mom gave us as kids?"

Jake's expression softens, a hint of nostalgia in his smile as he nods. "Yeah, those were the days."

Jake chuckles, the sound deep and warm, making my insides flutter. "Remember when we nearly set the kitchen on fire trying to make those damn cookies?"

I laugh, the memory vivid. "Oh god, yes. Your mom was so pissed. I thought she was going to ban me from the house forever."

"Nah, she could never stay mad at you." Jake's gaze turns tender. "No one could. You've always had a way of wrapping people around your little finger."

I swallow hard, my mouth suddenly dry. The way Jake is looking at me, with such raw intensity, makes my pulse race. I lick my lips nervously and his eyes darken as they zero in on the movement. The air between us feels electric, charged with a tension I've never felt before.

I've got to be imagining things. This is Jake…

So, I shake it off and act like everything's normal.

Because everything is normal, right?

Jake

I watch as Lily absently twirls a strand of her golden hair around her finger, a faraway look in her blue eyes. "So, there's this guy I've been seeing lately," she says, her voice deceptively casual. "Nothing serious, but it's been nice to get out there again, you know?"

A sudden, hot surge of jealousy coils in my gut. My hands clench into fists beneath the table. I takes a slow breath, fighting to keep my expression neutral as my heart falls. "Oh yeah? That's great, Lil. I'm happy for you." The words taste like ash on my tongue.

Lily shrugs, a small smile playing at the corners of her mouth. "Like I said, it's nothing major. Just a few dates here and there. But he's sweet, and it's been fun."

I nods mechanically, my mind reeling. The thought of another man touching Lily, kissing her, holding her...it's almost too much to bear. I wants to grab her by the shoulders, to shake her and shout that can't she see what's right in front of her? That I'm not just her childhood pal or her surrogate brother—I'm a man who wants her with every fiber of his being.

But I remain silent, my jaw clenched so tightly it aches. "That's good," I manage, but the words sound stilted and hollow to my own ears. "You deserve to be happy, Lily."

Even as I say it, a traitorous voice whispers in the back of my mind. *She could be happy with you. Happier than she'll ever be with some random guy who doesn't know her like you do, who doesn't love her like you do.*

I swallow hard, shoving down the possessive thoughts that threaten to consume me. Lily is my best friend, and her happiness is all that matters.

But I'm not sure I can watch her find that happiness with someone else.

six

. . .

Jake

THE MOONLIGHT FILTERING through the window catches in Lily's blonde hair as she leans against my shoulder, her soft curves pressing into my side. I stare out at the night sky, trying to ignore the heat of her body and focus on the stars. But it's impossible.

"Do you ever wonder what else is out there?" Lily asks, her voice barely above a whisper. "If there's more to life than...this?"

She gestures vaguely at the quiet street. I know what she means though. This town, these routines.

She shakes her head and chuckles, "But of

course you know. You've traveled and seen some of the world as a Marine."

I shrug. "Nothing is as good as being back here," I murmur.

I risk a glance down at her. Lily's blue eyes shine in the dim light, full of dreams she's never shared with anyone else. Anyone but me.

My heart pounds against my ribs. I could tell her. I could say that I wonder about a life with her, about holding her, *loving* her. The words rise in my throat.

"Lily, I..."

She turns to me, lips parted. I'm drowning in the endless blue of her eyes.

"I think maybe we're meant for bigger things sometimes," I say instead. A coward to the end.

Lily nods, unaware of my racing pulse. "I want that. Adventure. Romance. I want to fall in love so deeply it consumes me."

I clench my hands into fists. I want to consume her, to brand her as mine and never let her go.

"You'll have that someday," I manage to get out.

She smiles, and it's radiant. I'd go to war all over again to keep that smile on her face.

"Speaking of romance," Lily says, "I have to tell you about this date I went on last week!"

And just like that, the moment fractures. She

gushes about some guy who took her to dinner, and I make the right noises at the right times. All the while, I'm trapped in the prison of my own making.

And all I can wonder is if she's still a virgin.

My hands ball into fists at the thought of someone else touching her.

So close to what I want most, and still so far. With Lily warm against my side, smelling like sunshine incarnate, her voice washing over me as she shares her excitement over another man.

Slowly, silently, I bleed.

seven

· · ·

Jake

I'M FROZEN IN PLACE, my heart threatening to shatter as I watch Lily smile at her date across the restaurant table. She looks radiant, her blue eyes sparkling with laughter at something he said. It's a stab to my gut, seeing her so happy with someone else.

My fists clench at my sides. I want to storm over there, to yank her away from him, to claim her as *mine*.

But I have no right. I'm just her friend, the guy who's always been there for her but never had the courage to confess my true feelings.

The rational part of my brain tells me to walk away, to let her enjoy her evening. But the jealous beast inside me roars in protest. I can't stand seeing his hand reach across the table to touch hers. She's not his to touch. She's mi—

Lily angrily yanks her arm away as the guy grabs it more forcefully. In an instant, the leash on my control snaps.

I'm across the room before I can think, my hand fisting in the collar of his shirt as I haul him up from his chair. He sputters in shock as I sling him away from her.

"Don't you ever fucking touch her again," I snarl, my voice guttural and seething with barely contained violence. "You lay a hand on her, and I will end you. Do you understand me?"

The guy pales and nods frantically before scurrying away. I'm breathing hard, my pulse pounding in my ears as I turn back to Lily. Her blue eyes are wide with shock.

"Jake! What has gotten into you?" she demands.

"Why can't you look at me that way?" The words rip from my throat before I can stop them, raw and desperate.

Lily blinks, her brow furrowing in confusion. "What? Jake, what are you talking about?"

I stalk closer, my body vibrating with the need to make her understand. To make her *see* me. "The way you looked at him. Why can't you ever look at me like that?"

"Like what? Jake, you're not making any sense."

A growl rumbles in my chest. I'm done with words. Done pretending I don't burn for her with every breath.

I close the distance between us and crush my mouth against hers. Lily makes a startled sound, but I swallow it down, my tongue delving deep to taste her. God, she's sweet. Better than I ever imagined.

I pour years of pent-up longing into the kiss, my hands gripping her curvy waist to yank her flush against me. I need her closer. Need to feel every soft curve melded to my hardness.

Lily's hands come up to push at my chest, and I reluctantly tear my mouth away. We're both panting. Her lips are pink and swollen, her eyes dazed.

"Jake..." She looks shell-shocked.

"I'm in love with you," I rasp. "I have been for years. I can't watch you with someone else. Not anymore."

Her mouth falls open. "You...you love me? But we're friends..."

"I don't want to be just your friend, Lily. I want to be everything to you. I want you to be *mine*."

I smash my lips back onto her desperately, willing her to see the depth of my emotions.

If I can't put it into words, I'll show her.

She has to understand…

eight

. . .

Lily

JAKE'S LIPS crash into mine and everything else fades away. His strong hands grip my waist, pulling me flush against his hard body as his mouth devours me with a hunger I've never known.

Sparks ignite under my skin, desire pooling low in my belly. Holy crap, no kiss has ever felt like this!

I melt into him, my fingers threading through his short hair to hold him close. A desperate moan escapes me as his tongue delves deep, claiming me, possessing me.

I'm drowning in sensation, in *Jake*. My best friend. The man I never dared to dream could want me this way.

He breaks the kiss to trail his lips along my jaw, his breath hot against my ear. "Lily...god, I've wanted this for so long. Wanted you."

His deep, rumbling words send shivers down my spine. I'm panting, trembling in his arms, aching for more of his touch. "Jake..." It's the only coherent thought I can form.

Suddenly I'm airborne as he scoops me up, one arm under my knees and the other supporting my back. Our eyes lock, the blistering heat in his green depths stealing my breath. He strides purposefully out of the bar, each step jostling me against his muscular chest.

The night air is cool on my flushed skin but does nothing to calm the inferno raging inside me. Jake's mouth finds mine again as he carries me down the street and into his apartment building. I'm only vaguely aware of the journey, too lost in his drugging kisses.

He kicks the door shut behind us, and I know there's no going back. I'm about to cross a line with my best friend that I can never uncross.

And I don't care.

I want him with every fiber of my being. I need him like I need air.

He stops us in the middle of his dimly lit bedroom, pressing me against the wall. His emerald eyes drill into mine as his hands trail up my thighs, lifting my skirt to my waist. "I've been waiting for this day, Lily. I've fantasized about this moment a thousand times."

His words send a thrill straight to my core. "Jake, I never knew you..."

"Shh, Lily, let me show you."

His fingers make short work of my lace panties, and then there's nothing between us but our burning skin. My body aches for him as he grinds his hips against mine, his erection hard and insistent against my center. "So wet, baby," he groans into my ear, sending shivers down my spine. "You feel so damn good."

"Jake...god, I...I...," I stutter incoherently, overwhelmed by the sensations coursing through me.

He kisses a trail of blazing heat down my neck, stopping just above my cleavage. "You're all mine tonight, Lily. Every perfect, curvy inch of you." His possessive growl sends a visceral thrill through me. "Tell me you're mine."

"Yours, Jake...I'm yours," I moan, arching my back to feel more of him.

"And do you know what's mine?" he growls, nibbling on my earlobe.

"T-tell me," I pant out.

"Every. Fucking. Inch. You were always meant to be mine, Lily. Every beautiful, curvy part of you." His hands splay across my hips, as if to emphasize his point.

Unable to form a coherent reply, I moan in response as he teases my hardened nipple with his tongue. It's too much, the pleasure coursing through me, and I'm on the verge of orgasm before he even breaches me.

"Oh, Jake, please..." I whimper, my hips grinding against his hard length. "I...I need you."

"I got you, babe," he whispers, his voice a low rumble that sets my nerves on fire.

He pushes a finger into me and then stills when he feels my hymen. His eyes darken as he chokes out, "You're still a virgin, Lil?"

My cheeks color with embarassment as I nod. "Well, yeah. I mean, you're my best friend. I'd have told you if I lost it."

"Thank fuck," he growls. "Do you know how many nights the thought of another man claiming what's mine has tortured me?"

My heart starts beating faster at his possessive

words. Fuck, but I love how possessive Jake is being.

He whispers, his voice hot in my ear. "Do you know how long I've jacked off to the thought of you?"

I gasp. Why does that admission send moisture flooding between my thighs?

He crashes his lips back onto mine, and then with one swift motion, he plunges into me, shredding my virginity and filling me completely.

I gasp, my nails digging into his back as the sensation of being claimed by him washes over me.

"You feel so good, Lily. So fucking tight." Jake's grip on my hips tightens, his hips starting a relentless, pounding rhythm. "God, I've wanted you for so long...needed this...you..."

I can only moan in response, lost in the sensations he's creating within me.

"Lily...sweet Lily...love you...love..." His words taper off as his thrusts become even more urgent, pulling me along with him into a maelstrom of pleasure.

My world shatters into a million shimmering pieces as an explosive orgasm rips through me, my inner walls clenching around Jake's thick shaft buried deep inside me. "Jake! Oh god, Jake!" I cry out, clinging to him as wave after wave of ecstasy crashes over me.

"That's it, baby. Come for me," he growls, his hips slamming into mine, prolonging my release. "Fucking perfect...my perfect Lily..."

His words, his rough possession, the feel of him pulsing inside me—it's all too much. I shatter again, my body spasming uncontrollably around him as a second orgasm overtakes me before the first has even subsided.

"Jake...Jake...fuck!" I moan incoherently, my nails scoring down his back. The coil inside me winds tighter and tighter with each forceful thrust until it finally snaps. I scream his name as pure, unadulterated bliss consumes me.

"Lily!" Jake roars. His hips jerk erratically as he finds his own release, spilling deep inside me with a guttural groan. "Lily, fuck!"

I cling to him, my legs locked around his waist, my inner walls still fluttering and milking his pulsing cock. Our heavy breaths mingle as we ride out the aftershocks together, lost in a haze of pleasure and passion.

Jake rests his forehead against mine, his intense green eyes boring into me. "I love you, Lily. I've always fucking loved you," he rasps, his voice raw with emotion as he pulls me on top of him and holds me tightly, stroking my head until we drift off to sleep together.

nine

· · ·

Jake

I ROLL OVER IN BED, reaching for Lily's warmth, but my hand meets only cold sheets. My eyes snap open, heart lurching in my chest as I realize she's gone. Sitting up, I glance around the empty room, her clothes no longer scattered across the floor where we left them in our heated frenzy last night.

Did she regret what we did? Did I come on too strong, scare her away with the intensity of my feelings that have been building for so long? I grab my phone from the nightstand, fingers shaking slightly as I type out a message.

> Hey, where'd you go? Everything okay?

I stare at the screen, each second that ticks by without a response twisting my stomach into tighter knots. Finally, after what feels like an eternity, her reply comes through.

> I'm sorry, I just need some time and space to process everything. Last night was...a lot. I'll call you in a few days.

A few days. The words stare back at me, taunting. How am I supposed to endure days without seeing her, touching her, after everything we shared? I want to tell her I love her, that she's all I've ever wanted, fuck her into submission.

But I know my Lily. I have to give her the space she's asking for, no matter how much it tears me apart.

The following days are absolute torture. Every text I begin typing, I delete. Every time I pick up the phone to call her, I lose my nerve. I go through the motions—eat, sleep, work out—but she consumes my every thought. The ghost of her scent lingers on my pillows. Memories of her body pressed against mine, her soft sighs and breathless moans, play on repeat in my mind.

I see her everywhere—in the cafe where we used to grab coffee, walking past the bookstore she loves to browse, in the park where we would picnic together in high school. But she's never actually there. It's like she's vanished from my life completely, leaving a gaping hole in her wake.

By the third day, I'm a wreck, pacing my apartment like a caged animal. I alternate between anger—at myself for risking our friendship, at her for running—and despair that I've lost her for good. She's embedded herself so deeply in my heart over the years, I don't know how to untangle her, to imagine a future without her by my side.

My phone buzzes and I practically lunge for it, praying it's her. But it's just my mom, checking in. I toss the phone aside in frustration, collapsing back onto the couch.

"Fuck," I mutter, dragging a hand down my face.

I'm in turmoil, caught between giving Lily the distance she needs and the overwhelming urge to show up at her door, drop to my knees, and beg her not to shut me out. I've never felt so powerless, so unmoored.

Still more days crawl by with no word from Lily. Each morning I wake with a jolt, grabbing for my phone, only to find silence. The disappointment is a constant ache in my chest, growing sharper with every day with no word.

I throw myself into work, punishing runs, anything to keep my mind off her. But she's always there, haunting my thoughts. The softness of her skin, the raw vulnerability in her eyes that night—it consumes me.

Doubt begins to fester, seeping into the cracks of my mind. What if I pushed too hard, moved too fast? What if I've lost her for good?

The fear that goes through me at the thought is paralyzing.

Late one sleepless night, whiskey burning in my veins, I break. My fingers tremble as I type out the words I swore I'd never say.

> I'm sorry, Lil. I never meant to put this on you, to risk what we have. Just tell me we're going to be okay. That I haven't lost you. I'll try to go back to being just friends if that's what you want, but I can't lose you.

I stare at the screen until the letters blur, thumb hovering over send.

I can't send it.

Every instinct screams to fix this, to fight for her. But I can't be that selfish. Slowly, I delete the text, each press of my finger an agony.

I hurl my glass against the wall, watching it shatter. The anger drains out of me in a rush, leaving me hollow. Defeated, I slump back on the couch, head in my hands.

Loving her is the easiest thing I've ever done. But if I've ruined us because I couldn't keep that love locked away... that's a guilt I'll carry forever. All I can do is hope that fifteen years of friendship is stronger than one night of passion. Strong enough to bring her back to me, in whatever way she's able to be in my life.

Anything's better than losing her completely.

ten

· · ·

Lily

I STARE out at the shimmering lake, wrapped in the emerald embrace of towering pines. Our initials are still etched into the weathered bark of our tree, faded but indelible like the bond we share. Memories flood back, sparking a revelation that rocks me to my core.

It makes sense now, why I could never truly give myself to anyone else. Why I always found something wrong with every guy I ever dated.

They weren't *him*.

I've always loved Jake. Not just as my best friend, but with a deep, aching desire I never dared name. Fear held me captive, terrified that by reaching for more, I'd lose the one person who knows me better than I know myself.

My pulse races as I hear the crunch of footsteps behind me. I turn to see Jake emerging from the shadowed forest path, his chiseled face a mask of anguish.

"Lily..." My name is a tormented whisper on his lips. "I had to find you. To see you, even if it's the last time."

His pain pierces me like shards of glass. I take a step towards him, my voice trembling. "Jake, I could never shut you out. You're a part of me."

Emotions war across his handsome features—desperation, longing, regret. "I've been such a fool, Lily. Hiding what's in my heart, convinced I'd ruin everything between us."

Tears sting my eyes as understanding dawns. He loves me too. Has always loved me, just as I've loved him.

I close the distance between us, gently cupping his face in my hands. "You could never ruin us, Jake. We've been through too much, are too deeply connected."

His eyes search mine, a crackling intensity in their green depths. I see the moment he realizes the truth. That I'm his, heart and soul, just as he is mine.

Jake pulls me flush against his hard body, strong arms banding around me like steel. "I love you, Lily," he rasps against my hair. "I've loved you my entire life. I just never dreamed you might feel the same."

My fingers curl into his shirt, anchoring me as a wave of pure joy crashes over me. "I do feel the same, Jake. I just didn't realize it until now, and I'm sorry for running. It was just…so overwhelming and kinda scary."

He pulls back just enough to meet my gaze, his expression fierce with possessiveness. "You never need to be afraid of this, of us. I'm yours, baby. Always have been."

I nod, my lips trembling on a shaky exhale. "And I'm yours. I don't want to waste another second pretending this connection between us isn't everything."

His mouth claims mine in a searing kiss, telling me without words that he intends to spend the rest of his life showing me exactly what *everything* means.

I surrender to the heated slide of his lips, the intoxicating taste of him, as my heart soars with the knowledge that this is just the beginning for us.

When he finally releases me, we're both breathing hard, the air around us electric. "No more holding back," he vows gruffly.

"No more hiding," I agree breathlessly.

Under the branches of our tree, we make a new promise. One based not on fear or doubt, but on the bone-deep certainty of a love that has always been the core of who we are. Together.

Slowly, Jake unties the ribbon that's been holding my dress together, his movements deliberate and reverent. The fabric pools around my ankles, leaving me naked before him in more ways than one. But I've never felt more exposed or more safe than in this moment.

He doesn't say a word as he takes in the sight of my body, but his eyes speak volumes. Desire, hunger, and most of all, tenderness. It's enough to make my knees buckle if it weren't for the support of the tree I'm leaning against.

"You're so fucking beautiful, Lily." His voice is rough with emotion, his hands shaking as he gently caresses my curves. "I've dreamed of this for as long as I can remember."

A blush creeps up my chest, but I don't look away. I want him to see me—all of me.

He growls low in his throat, animalistic and primal. "You have no idea how much I want you," he whispers, his hands sliding higher, cupping my breasts. "I'm going to spend every day of the rest of our lives claiming every inch of this gorgeous body and making you mine."

"Then do it, Jake," I beg, arching my back and inviting his touch. "I'm yours. I've always been yours."

With a groan of pleasure and frustration, he undresses himself, revealing his hard length. My mouth waters as I take in the sight of him, so strong and virile, and aching for me.

"God, Lily. I need you." He steps closer, his hips aligning with my wet folds. "Tell me you're mine. I need to hear your say it again."

"I'm yours, Jake. Always and forever." I wrap my legs around his waist, drawing him closer.

He doesn't hesitate any longer. With a primal growl, he pushes into me, claiming me as his own. I gasp, arching my back as I take him in—all of him. It's a perfect fit, like we were made for each other.

"You feel so good, Lily," he moans, his eyes wild with desire. "So fucking tight and wet for me."

"Jake," I moan back, nails digging into his back as he thrusts in and out of me, his movements building a blinding pleasure within me. "Oh God, I love you, Jake."

"I love you too, Lily," he pants, his thrusts becoming more urgent. "I've always loved you."

As our bodies move together in harmony, the world around us fades away. There's no war, no danger, no secrets—only us, two people who have finally found their way back to each other.

"I'm close, Lily. I'm gonna—" Jake throws his head back with a groan, and I feel him explode inside of me, flooding me with his warmth.

"Jake!" I cry out, my own climax overtaking me, my body shuddering around his.

In the afterglow, we hold each other tightly, our bodies still joined, our rapid breaths mingling in the cool night air.

"I love you, Lily. So much" Jake whispers, his voice husky with emotion.

"I love you too, Jake. So much," I smile, my heart full to the brim.

Jake is my everything. My best friend and the love of my life.

epilogue

. . .

Three years later

Jake

I WALK through the front door after a long day on base, my combat boots thudding on the hardwood floor. The smells of roasting garlic and fresh bread envelop me, welcoming me home.

"Daddy's home!" Lily calls out in a singsong voice from the kitchen. I hear the patter of little feet and our two-year-old son appears, toddling towards me with chubby arms outstretched.

"There's my little man," I say, scooping him up

and burying my nose in his soft blond curls. He smells like baby shampoo and pure innocence.

Lily emerges from the kitchen, her pregnant belly straining against the flowery apron tied around her waist. Even with flour smudged on her cheek, no makeup, and her hair piled in a messy bun, she takes my breath away. Pregnancy has only made her more radiant, her skin glowing and breasts fuller. My beautiful, perfect wife.

I set our son down and he toddles off to play. Lily steps into my open arms and I pull her flush against me, as close as her swollen belly will allow. I capture her lips in a deep, possessive kiss.

"Mmm, I missed you today," she murmurs against my mouth. "Dinner's almost ready."

"I'm hungry for something else," I growl, nipping at her lower lip. My hands roam her lush curves, squeezing her round ass. "You look so fucking sexy, baby. Carrying my child...I can't get enough of you."

She giggles and swats my chest. "Jake! Language. Little ears," she scolds, but her blue eyes sparkle with amusement and desire.

I back her up against the wall, pinning her there with my hips. "I need you, and don't pretend you're not an insatiable little minx who can't keep her hands off her husband." Something I really love about her.

I slip a hand under her apron and cup her breast, thumbing the pebbled nipple through thin cotton. She arches into me with a breathy gasp. "Can you blame me? I'm so horny all the time."

My other hand slides between her thighs, under her skirt. I groan when I find her bare and already slick with arousal. "Christ, Lily. You trying to kill me?"

I rub tight circles over her swollen clit and she mewls, clutching at my shoulders. "Only a little death, Marine."

I want to bend her over the couch and bury myself in her wet heat, but the oven timer dings. Lily wiggles out of my arms with a breathless laugh.

"Hold that thought. Let me get dinner on the table first."

I watch her ass sway as she walks back to the kitchen, adjusting myself in my fatigues. Never in my wildest dreams did I imagine having this—Lily as my wife, our perfect son, another baby on the way, the white picket fence. But here we are, all her dreams come true.

And later, after our boy is sleeping soundly, I'll show her just how much I cherish her. I'll worship my sweet Lily, the mother of my children. I'll map every inch of her skin with hands and mouth, claim her body once again as she so eagerly surrenders.

I'll fill her up, leave her sated and dripping with my seed. My perfect bride, round with my child.

Forever *mine*.

We eat dinner, and I swear she's teasing me. The way she slowly licks her fork, sliding it out of her mouth and staring at me with those bedroom eyes…

———

Lily

I know exactly what I'm doing to Jake, licking my fork like that, letting it slowly slide from between my pursed lips. His green eyes darken and he shifts in his seat, no doubt imagining that tongue on his cock instead.

"Mm, this is so good, baby," I moan appreciatively, taking another bite of the garlic bread. "You want a taste?"

I hold out a morsel to him, and he leans in to

take it between his teeth, lips brushing my finger-tips. I shiver at the contact.

The heat in his gaze makes my core clench with need. I squirm in my seat, rubbing my thighs together to get some friction where I'm throbbing for him.

He gives me a look that promises revenge.

Good. I can't wait.

After we put our little man to bed, Jake stalks towards me with a predatory gleam in his eye. He backs me into our bedroom, kicking the door shut behind him.

"You teased me all through dinner, you naughty girl," he growls, crowding me against the wall. "Flashing me glimpses of your creamy thighs, licking your lips like you're starving for my cock." He nuzzles into my neck, nipping and sucking at the sensitive skin. "Teasing me with this lush body ripe with my baby."

His large hands roam my curves possessively, cupping my heavy breasts. He rolls my nipples between his fingers and I gasp, arching into his touch. "Jake, please..."

"Please what, sweet girl? Tell me what you need."

"I need you inside me. I'm so empty." I practically sob the words, writhing against him desperately.

I don't know what it is. I've always been horny for Jake, but being pregnant has shot my hormones into overdrive.

I'm *insatiable*.

He hikes up my skirt and practically rips my panties off me, the flimsy lace no match for his Marine strength. I whimper as cool air hits my overheated flesh, already so slick and ready for him.

"Fuck, baby, you're dripping," he groans, fingers delving into my sodden folds. I cry out when he circles my aching clit, hips bucking into his touch. "This hungry little pussy is all mine. No one else gets to see you like this, so desperate and wanton."

"Yes, only yours!" I agree frantically, dizzy with need. "Please, Jake..."

He brings his fingers to my mouth, coated in my juices. "Suck."

I open obediently and he pushes his fingers inside. I moan around the digits, laving them with my tongue, tasting my own musky arousal. His eyes burn into me, dark with lust.

"On the bed. Now," he commands gruffly. "I'm going to feast on this sweet cunt before I fuck you senseless."

A thrill races through me and I scramble to obey, climbing onto our king-sized bed. He prowls after me like a wolf stalking his prey. I start to lay back, but he stops me with a hand on my hip.

"No. On your hands and knees." His voice is rough, sending shivers down my spine. "I want to see my baby in your belly."

I position myself as he asked, knees spread wide, my heavy tits hanging down. He kneels behind me, big hands smoothing over the globes of my ass appreciatively.

"Fucking perfect," he praises, landing a light slap on one cheek. I yelp, then moan as he soothes the sting with his palm. "Round with my child, ass in the air for me like a bitch in heat."

His filthy words make me clench around nothing. I'm shamefully aroused by his degradation, by him putting me in my place as his broodmare, the receptacle for his seed.

"Please, Jake, I need your mouth on me," I whine, wiggling my hips invitingly.

He spreads me open, dragging a long lick through my folds and over my tight little pucker. I keen, pushing back against his face. He laps at me, circling my clit, fucking into my channel with his tongue.

"Oh god, yes, just like that! Ah!" My arms give

out and I face-plant into the mattress, ass still high in the air. He redoubles his efforts, sucking my clit into his mouth as he plunges two thick fingers knuckle-deep into my weeping core.

It only takes moments before I'm flying apart with a scream of his name, my walls clamping down on his plundering fingers.

I cry out his name as the pleasure crashes over me, my entire body quaking with the force of my release. Jake doesn't let up, his fingers and tongue relentlessly stoking the flames, pushing me higher until I'm sobbing from the intensity.

"That's it, baby, come on my tongue," he growls against my dripping flesh. "Fucking drown me."

I do, gushing into his eager mouth as a second orgasm rips through me, even more powerful than the first. Spots dance behind my eyelids and I collapse fully onto the bed, boneless.

Jake gentles his touch, lapping softly at my sensitized flesh, licking me clean of my release. I whimper and twitch as little aftershocks zing through my nerve endings.

"You taste so goddamn good," he rumbles appreciatively. "I could eat this pussy for hours."

I mewl at his words, exhausted but still needy. I need him inside me, stretching me, filling me up.

As if reading my mind, Jake flips me over onto

my back and settles his hips between my splayed thighs. His green eyes are wild and hungry as they rove over my body laid out before him like a feast.

My heavy breasts, nipples straining against the confines of my bra. My rounded belly, ripe with his child. The wet and swollen flesh of my bare pussy, pink and glistening from his oral attentions.

"Fucking look at you," he rasps, voice gravelly with lust. "All mine. My perfect little wife."

"Yes, yours," I breathe, reaching for him. "Please, Jake, I need you inside me. I'm aching."

He curses under his breath and practically rips his fatigues open, shoving them down just enough to free his straining erection. I lick my lips at the sight of him, so hard and thick, the bulbous head an angry purple and weeping precum.

Jake notches himself at my entrance and surges forward, hilting inside me with one powerful thrust. I keen at the sudden penetration, my inner muscles fluttering around his invading length. No matter how many times he takes me, I'm always so tight for him.

"Fuck, Lily, you feel incredible," he grunts, pulling out slowly and slamming back in. "Hot and slick and gripping me so good. Like this pussy was made for me."

"It was," I moan, wrapping my legs high around

his waist, opening myself up even more. "Only for you, Jake. Forever."

He sets a relentless pace, pounding into me hard and deep, just the way I need it. The wet, obscene sounds of flesh meeting flesh fill the room, punctuated by our gasps and groans of pleasure.

Jake dips his head and captures one of my nipples in his mouth.

His mouth is hot and demanding on my breast, tongue swirling around the sensitive peak. I tangle my fingers in his short hair, holding him to me as he suckles greedily.

"God, Jake, yes!" I moan, my back arching off the bed. The dual sensations of his mouth on my nipple and his thick cock plundering my needy channel send sparks of ecstasy zinging through my body.

He releases my breast with a wet pop and kisses his way up my chest, my neck, capturing my mouth in a searing kiss. I can taste myself on his tongue and it only inflames my desire.

Pulling back, he braces his weight on his forearms on either side of my head, his hips still churning, driving into me with deep, purposeful strokes. His intense green eyes bore into mine, dark with possession and carnal hunger.

"You take my cock so well, baby," he rasps, voice

rough with strain. "Fucking made for it. Made for me to fill this sweet cunt with my seed over and over."

I clench around him at his filthy words, my pussy weeping copiously, easing his way. "Yes, Jake, fill me up!" I keen desperately, my nails raking down his back. "Breed me again, give me another baby!"

He curses harshly and redoubles his efforts, fucking into me with wild abandon. The headboard slams against the wall with each powerful thrust. "Fuck, Lily, you want that? Want me to put another bun in this oven?"

"Yes, god yes!" I babble mindlessly, drunk on pleasure. "I want to be big and round with your babies, all the time!"

The idea of him keeping me constantly pregnant, my belly and breasts always swollen with his children, my body perpetually soft and ripe for his taking, sends me hurtling towards the edge.

"I'm so close, Jake! Don't stop, please don't stop!" I wail, my thighs beginning to shake, my stomach muscles quivering and tightening.

He hammers into me, grinding his pelvis against my aching clit with every thrust. "That's it, baby, come on my cock," he commands gruffly.

"Squeeze the cum out of me, milk me dry. Fucking take it!"

His words are my undoing. I detonate with a silent scream, my orgasm crashing over me in waves of mind-numbing ecstasy. My cunt clamps down on him rhythmically, rippling along his pistoning length.

Jake stiffens above me, his hips stuttering. "Fuck, Lily, fuck!" he roars, slamming into me one last time and exploding, painting my insides with his hot release.

I moan at the feel of him throbbing and spurting deep inside me, his potent seed flooding my womb.

I milk his cock with my fluttering inner muscles, drawing out every last drop. Our mingled fluids seep out around his softening shaft, making a sticky mess between my thighs.

Jake collapses on top of me, his weight pressing me into the mattress. I welcome the crush of his body, enveloping me, anchoring me. He nuzzles into my neck with a contented rumble.

"I love you," he murmurs against my sweat-dampened skin. "So fucking much."

My heart swells at his words, tears pricking the corners of my eyes. "I love you too, Jake. More than anything."

We lay there tangled together, basking in the afterglow. His hand smooths over the swell of my belly reverently. "I can't wait to meet this little one," he says, voice filled with wonder. "See what other perfect blend of us we've created."

"Me too," I whisper, covering his hand with my own. The life we've built together, this family, is beyond my wildest dreams. I'm so incredibly blessed.

Jake shifts off of me and spoons up behind my back, one strong arm banding across my chest. He splays his other hand across my rounded stomach possessively. "Sleep, my sweet wife."

I hum in agreement, exhaustion pulling at me. I snuggle back into his warm bulk, feeling cherished and protected. Safe.

"Love you," I slur, already drifting.

The last thing I feel before sleep claims me is the soft press of his lips against my hair and his deep, rumbling voice.

"Love you, Lily. Always."

Want a free book from Emma Bray? Go to www. authoremmabray.com.

. . .

Keep reading for an excerpt from Soldier's Symphony.

Harper

"Oh, come on, Harper! You have to go with us!"

Meg is looking up at me with her big blue eyes. She widens them so they look like puppy dog eyes and pouts as she begs. "It'll be so much fun! I promise you. All you ever do is work. You need to get out and live a little."

I sigh. Meg's got me there. Ever since my dad died, all I've done is work. Of course, I do it to make ends meet, but I've also taken on extra shifts —as many as I can to keep busy.

My dad left me the little bungalow where I grew up. He was smart enough to make sure the house was completely paid off long ago, so it's not like I have a mortgage or rent to worry about. I just have to pay my electric bill and taxes and buy my food and necessities.

Most of what I'm earning now goes into a small savings account. I don't know what I'm saving up for. My dreams died the day my dad did. I just don't have the passion for anything I used to anymore.

I finish wiping down my table while Meg continues to flutter around me like a butterfly. "All the other waitresses are going," she adds. "Molly and Mary will be there. And even Chrissy."

I try not to wrinkle up my nose at the mention of Chrissy, though I can tell by Meg's face that she's not exactly thrilled Chrissy will be there either.

Chrissy acts like she's better than the rest of us and makes it clear every time she steps through the doors that she doesn't need this job. She's just doing it to make extra money before she goes to college.

Besides Chrissy, I get along well with all of my co-workers, especially Meg, who barnacled herself onto me the moment I walked in the door. She decided I needed a friend and applied herself generously to that role.

Growing up as an only child, I didn't have a lot of friends. It was always just my dad and me. I'm a little on the quiet side. I'm not exactly shy, but I never saw the need to be the life of the party. I was the kind of girl who could talk to my classmates and get along well with all of them. I was pretty well-liked, but I wasn't particularly close to anyone.

But none of that matters now that we're all

grown up. I'm waiting tables here at the diner, and only God knows what the rest of them are doing. If I had to bet, I would guess most of them are in college now. Many of my classmates were trust fund babies.

I honestly don't know how my dad could afford to send me to private school, but he insisted that I get a good education in a safe environment.

My heart wrenches at the thought of him. It's been two years, yet I still miss him like it was yesterday. He was my best friend.

I never knew my mother. She died giving birth to me, but my father never held that against me—even when I held it against myself. He told me that I was her pride and joy when she was pregnant and that she wouldn't have regretted her sacrifice. Dad also assured me that she'd be so proud of the woman I'd become.

Meg's face falls as if she can tell the turn my thoughts have taken. Meg is a good friend. She's been here for me through it all.

The day I got the phone call that my dad was in a bad car crash, she was the one who held me while I cried. She knows firsthand what I've been through. She was there to wrap her arms around me when I needed someone to cry on, and I'll forever be grateful to her for that.

I'm not into all this social stuff, though. After a long day at work, I like to go home and relax by myself with a good book or a movie, but I know my friend means well. She just worries about me.

That's why I hear myself agreeing. "Sure, Meg. Count me in."

"Sweet!" she squeals as she flutters off to get back to work.

I smile to myself. Maybe it will be good for me to get out for a night with the girls.

———

The girls don't take me to a rambunctious club, and for that, I'm thankful. I'm so not into the club scene. Instead, we hit up a local bar where the vibe is good, and there's no pressure to dance and gyrate all over one another like there is at a club.

We're all dressed pretty casually in skirts and tank tops, but nothing outrageous.

I instantly relax as we drink a few flirty cocktails and the girls' chatter. They talk about some of our usual customers, and Meg makes this hilarious impression of one of our grumpiest regulars that has us all laughing.

I grip my stomach with deep belly laughs—the kind that I haven't experienced in years. It's the kind of laugh that makes your stomach hurt but in a good way. I wipe the tears from my eyes. Meg was right. This feels good. Yes, I still miss my dad, but I know he wouldn't want me to grieve for him forever. He would want me to have friends and start living again.

So, I vow to myself that's what I'm going to do.

We're a couple of drinks in when people start going up on the stage for to sing karaoke. Unsurprisingly, Chrissy is the first one in our group to volunteer. We all giggle and clap supportively. She's not as good a singer as she thinks she is, but she's not horrible, either. She's just a little over the top.

"Okay, now it's your turn, Harper." Meg turns her big blue eyes on me.

"Oh, no." I shake my head, my palms sweating at the thought of getting on the stage in front of a bunch of people—even if they are people I don't know.

"Yes, you have to!" Molly and Mary agree. "We'll go after you, but you go next."

"No, girls, I really don't want to," I protest, but Meg is already plucking my drink from my fingers and pulling me to stand.

"Harper, you're an amazing singer. You'll do great!" she tells me.

I give her a pleading look.

Yes, Meg has heard me sing. I used to love singing, but it's something I haven't done much of since my father died. That was kind of *our* thing. Dad played the guitar while I sang along with him. He loved to hear me sing. At one time, I even dreamed of going to music school and studying the vocal arts, but I gave all that up when Dad died. Just like I've pretty much given up singing.

Something I know my dad wouldn't want. He'd be so sad knowing I've stopped singing, and that thought cements my decision.

Meg continues to pull on my arm, and I finally concede. What the hell? So far, all of Meg's suggestions—like the one that I come out tonight—have turned out well. And I also vowed that I was going to let loose and live a little, so I'm just gonna go for it. Who cares if I bomb it, right? Everyone in this place is tipsy, and a lot of the people who've gotten up haven't been good singers. Karaoke is all in good fun anyway. It's not like we're seriously out to impress anyone.

"Okay, what are you going to sing, little lady?" the DJ manning the karaoke asks me with a wink.

I glance over at Meg. I don't have the first clue what to choose, but in true Meg fashion, she's ready to volunteer something.

I know the song she suggests, so I shrug at the DJ and go with it. It's not one of the campy, cheesy, upbeat songs, but it's not a slow song either. It's more of a rock-pop ballad—one that I remember singing a lot with my dad while he played the electric guitar.

I let the music wash over me. I haven't sung much in the past couple of years, but I still love to listen to music, losing myself in the chords and melodies.

I close my eyes when the song reaches the opening stanza. It's my cue to sing, so I take a deep breath, open my mouth, and let loose.

I get lost in the lyrics, lost in the melody. I'm singing from the bottom of my heart, remembering my father. This is like a cleansing, a revelation, as I silently dedicate this song to him.

I get so caught up in my song that I forget where I am. When I open my eyes, the bar is so silent you can hear a pin drop. My face immediately flushes.

Oh, my God, I must have been horrible.

Suddenly, everyone erupts into applause, standing to their feet like they're at an opera or something. People are hooting and hollering and cheering, and my face flushes even deeper.

I nod my head in a humble bow and leave the stage. When I walk back over to the table where the girls are sitting, Molly and Mary are typing furiously on their phones.

I glance over their shoulders as I pass by them and gasp when I see what they're up to. "Oh my god, you guys! You *cannot* post that!"

They took a video of me singing, and they're posting it online.

"Too late!" Molly chirps up at me as her finger presses the send button.

"Yeah, too late for me too!" Mary says with a huge grin.

I cover my face with my hands. I don't want to be all over the internet. I'm not good enough for all that.

"What's wrong?" Meg asks me. "You were freaking amazing!"

"No, I'm so out of practice!" I groan. "I didn't know you guys were taking a video!" I shoot them all a distressed glance.

"Babe, we weren't the only ones," Molly notes as she jerks her head toward the rest of the room where other people are on their phones.

My cheeks flame, and I catch Chrissy out of the corner of my eye. She's glaring at me with her arms crossed, no doubt pissed off that I've stolen her thunder. Great. All I need is for her to be pissed off at me and give me more attitude than she already does at work. I was hoping that tonight would bridge the gap between us, and I think it did until my performance right after hers. I should have known better.

A few people come over to say hi to us and gush about my performance, and I sit there blushing like the idiot I am, feeling awkward. I've never been one for the spotlight, but I have to admit this feels good. It feels good to sing again and to hear that people enjoyed it.

When I finally go home, I have a smile on my face. For the first time in two years, I'm not crying as I fall asleep.

————

Erik

I work my way through my business emails as I do every morning while the news plays in the background. Taking a sip of my black coffee, I scowl at my computer screen. Fucking Donovan. It's always something with him. I type out a quick reply before I hit "send."

I scoff when I see that Morta has made yet another bid for one of my compositions. He may as well give it up. I'll never sell my work to anyone.

My music is my life. It's personal. It's not for public use. He should consider himself lucky that I fund his little musical theater.

I realize that I'm a bit backward. Most composers want the world to hear their work and love it, but I'm just the opposite. I hoard my compositions close to my chest like a dragon hoards treasure. I'm greedy. I don't want to share them with anyone. I think part of the reason is I know that no one else will be able to do my pieces justice.

I take another sip of my brew before something on the television catches my eye. I don't know why I turn the news on every morning. I rarely watch it, but now and then, a clip will catch my attention.

But nothing has ever caught my attention like this.

There's a girl on the screen. She has a thin build and long chocolate curls that flow down to her waist. They frame her face, making her look cherubic, like something from one of those classical paintings.

Her eyes are closed, her dark lashes laying on her creamy-white cheeks. She's wearing a fluttery little black skirt and a sky-blue tank top that shows just a hint of skin between the hem of her shirt and the band of the skirt.

It's not the clothing that gets my attention, though. She's not scantily dressed, and while she's beautiful—the most beautiful little angel I've ever seen—it's not that either.

No, what gets my attention is the crystal pure sound pouring from her pink lips. She has perfect pitch, her voice smooth and sweet. I've never heard anything like it in all my thirty-one years. Her voice is purity itself. I can't tear my eyes from her.

She's innocence personified, and that voice…

I'm suddenly burning to know everything about her. Who is she?

As if the news anchor hears my unspoken question, she answers, "That's Harper Young, ladies and gentleman, the waitress who's singing went viral last night."

She goes on to tell the story of how she and her friends were hanging out at this bar when Harper got up to do a karaoke number. Her friends filmed her and put her on the internet, and now she's become an overnight sensation.

"Harper." I taste the syllables on my lips. Sweet Jesus, her name tastes like honey. I speak it again, claiming it as mine.

Something inside me clicks. I've never wanted anyone to perform my compositions, but I'm suddenly dying to hear my music on her lips. It's crystal clear, like I've had an epiphany. It's her. She's who I've been waiting for. This marvelous, wonderful girl. This little angel sent down from heaven.

I pause the scene and rewind it to play back the clip. I can't tear my eyes from her as I watch the emotion flood across her face and pour out into her voice. Even though she has her eyes closed, she puts more emotion into that one song than the most practiced of musicians.

My eyes rove over her from head to toe, desire coursing through my veins. I'm aroused for the first time in years. Well, I'm no monk. I've been taking care of my needs myself for a while now, but it's been a long time since any female has elicited such a reaction.

I jump from my desk, excitement coursing through my veins. I feel like I'll die if I don't get to her soon. I don't know what my plan is, but I take off toward my library door. I stop when my hand touches the doorknob, glancing to my right. My gaze is drawn there unbidden.

There's a mirror hanging in the corner of the room. I hate mirrors. I *hate* the fucking things, but I left this one up because it was my mother's. However, I put it in the most obscure location so I don't have to look at myself.

I look now and scoff as I raise my hand to my scarred visage. I trail my fingers over the mangled flesh on the right side of my face. Fortunately, my injury doesn't cause me much pain, but it scarred up the right half of my face, making me look like a monster.

I force myself to gaze upon my scarred face, my jaw hardening as reality comes crashing down upon me once again. I'm a monster now. I'm not the good-looking man I once was, the man who could saunter up to any female and ask her out with complete confidence.

I drop my hand from the doorknob and hunch my shoulders as I turn back toward my desk, dejected.

There's a reason I keep myself sequestered away from the rest of society. The mirror starkly reminds me of that fact. I don't know what came over me that I momentarily forgot.

My eyes flick back up to the screen where Harper's beautiful face is displayed. Yes, I do. This little songbird with the voice and face of an angel. She's what came over me. I want her so bad it's a physical ache. My chest tightens, and I pull in panting breaths.

It can never be, I remind myself. She's beautiful and whole, whereas I'm half the man I used to be. She wouldn't give a poor sap like me the time of day.

I ball my hands into fists and lean on my desk, my jaw clenched so tightly I'm surprised I don't break the fucker. The hopelessness of my situation crashes over me until I roar in fury and swipe everything from my desk, knocking my laptop and everything onto the floor to shatter.

Nostrils flared, I grapple for control, my chest heaving like the beast I am. Shame washes over me at losing control like this. I'm no longer fit for polite society. This just proves it. I'm not worthy of an angel like her.

I look back at the screen, my heart breaking into a thousand pieces as I rewind the clip and watch it over and over and over again, torturing myself with the purity that I can never have.

I spend the next few days finding out everything about Harper Young. I have the best private investigator money can buy pull her file, and I study everything contained within it. I study her harder than I studied any course in college. She's twenty-one and waiting tables at a hole-in-the-wall diner—such a waste for a girl with her kind of talent.

I rewatch the clip of her singing like a man possessed. Her voice is ingrained in my head forever. I hear it when I sleep. I see her image every time I close my eyes. She's there all around me.

My world is irrevocably changed, and nothing will ever be the same again.

I have my man watch her all day while she's at work. Everywhere she goes, I have him following her and sending me a live feed of what's going on. It's obsessive and crazy and over the top, but I don't give a damn.

Maybe I can't approach her on my own, but I'll make damn sure I keep my eyes on her. I can't explain it, but I have this insane need to know where she is at all times. I need to watch over her even though she has no clue I exist.

Her father passed away a couple of years ago, so she's all alone in this world. Anything could have happened to her in those years before I knew of her, but I vow that nothing will now because she has me silently watching over her, protecting her.

She'll never be alone again. Whether she knows it or not, I'll always be there in the shadows, her silent benefactor making sure she has anything she needs. My heart clenches painfully at the knowledge that's all I can ever be.

It's not about sex, although I'd be lying if I said I'm not dying to sheath myself in her heat. No, it's more than that. My arms ache to hold her, stroke her like a little kitten. Talk to her and climb inside her mind to hear every thought in her beautiful head. Make all her dreams come true.

I certainly have the means to. I have all this money and no one to spend it on. What's the point in all of this if I have to do it alone? But I'm no longer alone because now I have a reason for living. I have Harper. I can take care of her, even if from afar.

I content myself with that until I turn on the TV one morning and see that Morta is on the morning news putting out a public offer for Harper to come work for him.

I drop my coffee cup, the hot beverage spilling onto my shirt and pants. It scalds me, but I barely feel the burn. My vision is blurring as panic seizes my chest.

There is no way in hell I'm going to let her work for another composer. I don't think I can bear for her to sing another man's compositions. The only songs she should be singing are mine.

I square my jaw with resolve.

When Harper sings, she's going to sing only for *me*.